WHAT WE TALK ABOUT WHEN WE TALK ABOUT LONELINESS

WHAT WE TALK ABOUT WHEN WE TALK ABOUT LONELINESS

Sai Tharun

PAPER TOWNS
PUBLISHERS

First published by

Papertowns Publishers

72, Vishwanath Dham Colony,
Niwaru Road, Jhotwara,
Jaipur, 302012

What We Talk About When We Talk About Loneliness

ISBN Print Book – 978-93-6185-046-2

Printed in India

Cover Design by Disha

Foreword

hen it comes to people and their emotions, for good or bad, I become a curious kid.

Of all the things that fascinate my childish brain, loneliness is the one that stands taller than all else. I've struggled for years trying to write something on loneliness. The concept proved too multi-faceted and multi-layered for me to get my thoughts in order to say everything I wanted to say.

Then, I watched a film "Stuck in Love". In that movie, the actor talked about a book, "What we talk about when we talk about love" by Raymond Carver.

I placed an order almost immediately.

I read that beaut of a book a week later and fell in love with it almost as inexplicably as I did with the concept of loneliness.

As I read that book, I realised why I was never able to write loneliness in one piece. Because, it's anything but one.

Loneliness is both subtle and obvious.
It's both tolerable and unbearable.

It's both self-serving and self-sabotaging. It
can open your eyes or eat your brain. It's
both unique and common.
Loneliness is complex in its simplicity.
Loneliness is what gives us love and takes it away.
Loneliness is our deepest fear.
Loneliness is what breaks us.
But maybe, if we understand it, it can make us. Just
maybe.

So, I took inspiration from the great Raymond Carver and
wrote this.

Here's what I (and hopefully, you) talk about when I (and
you too!) talk about loneliness.

Dedication

This book wouldn't be here if not for Mr. Raymond Carver, so I owe him a big thank you. I hope his soul is resting in peace knowing his words are inspiring people several generations later.

I also owe a whole lot of gratitude to my family, cousins and friends, who have all played a significant part in helping me understand the human condition. They have shaped me over the past 29 years. Neither I nor this book would be here if not for them and their beautiful hearts.

Gratitude is not sufficient, but it sure is necessary. So,

thank you, from the bottom of my heart.

Contents

Am I The Only One?

I was in school today and my friends were all talking about boys. They asked each other who their crush was. Everyone said a boy's name. When they asked me, I said I didn't have a crush on anyone. They thought I was lying.

"How can you not have a crush? Don't you like any guy? Do you not find John cute? Look at his hair. It looks so good!" they said.

But I didn't find any boy in my class or school attractive. In fact, I didn't find any hero attractive either. Yes, I thought some of them are handsome, but I was not physically attracted to any of them.

Today, when they asked me about my crush, I wanted to say the name of a senior. Her name is Priya. I've never seen someone as pretty as her. And you know what? She is so smart. And she is the school's best dancer. She can do everything. I really like her. But all the girls around me like boys. All boys like girls.

I knew that all the boys in school had a crush on Priya. If I had a crush on her, did that mean I was a boy? Did that mean something was wrong with me?

In all the movies I've watched, it's always a boy and a girl. It is never a girl and a girl, or a boy and a boy. Why is it so? Where do I find someone who can help me understand this?

All marriages are between boys and girls. Why are girls not married to each other?

I've had this confusion in my mind for more than a year. Whenever we watched a movie at home, all my female cousins talked about the hero. But I didn't want to talk about the hero. I wanted to talk about the heroine. I couldn't, because I was the only one who felt this way. I felt different. Did this make me odd? Should I feel like they do?

I wanted to think like they do. I didn't want to be different. What if they found out and stopped talking to me? What if my friends stopped playing with me? I was scared. How do I start liking boys? I didn't want to be different. I wanted to be like everyone else. Why was I the only one who felt this way?

Could I talk about this to someone? Will I be crucified if they knew how I felt? Was there something wrong with what I was feeling?

One afternoon, I couldn't take it anymore. I dragged my sister to our room and sat with her.

"I have to ask you something," I said.

"What is it?"

"Do you like boys?" I enquired.

"Yes. Why do you ask?" She smiled.

"Can I tell you a secret? Please promise me you won't tell anybody."

"Promise."

"I don't like boys. I like girls."

"I don't understand," she said, seeming confused.

"All my friends have crushes on boys. I have a crush on a girl"

"Ohh…"

"Is it wrong?"

My sister held my hand and pulled me into her chest. She was 10 years older than me and always took care of me.

She kissed me on top of my head, put her arms around me, and said, "it's not wrong, my darling girl".

I looked up and asked, "really?"

She nodded.

"So is it okay if I tell appa and amma? Will they be angry?"

"You told me. For now, let this remain a secret between sisters. When the time comes, I'll let you know what to do. Okay?"

"Okay," I said and hugged her tighter.

"Don't talk about this with anyone else, okay? Whatever doubts you have, you can ask me."

"Thank you."

I may be different. But at least there was someone who understood me. There was someone who didn't think I was weird, even though I did.

I cried that night, but not out of sadness. I cried because, for the first time, I didn't feel alone. For the first time, I felt a little normal. For the first time, I said something that felt criminal expecting to be chastised, but was accepted without ridicule.

I guess that's why they call older sisters a second mother.

Coffee ShOp

John liked sitting in a coffee shop for hours with a book in one hand and an Iced Tea in the other. He would let himself be consumed by the contents of the book. This evening, however, things felt different. He couldn't lose himself in the book. He put it down and looked around. He saw loads of people sitting from him, doing different things. He played music on his phone and began to observe each of them.

It was a Saturday evening with little else for him to do, so he decided to spend his time staring at random people in a crowded coffee shop and see what they were up to.

There was one young boy with headphones that looked super expensive at the last table at the very corner of the cafe. He was on his laptop doing something while simultaneously vibing to whatever was playing on his headphones. Was he a DJ, trying his mix on the laptop?

There was an awfully quiet couple. Both were on their mobile phones the entire time, hardly even looking at each other. Surely they could've done this at home, right? They didn't have to come out to a coffee shop to not look at each other, he thought. Anyway, that wasn't John's business.

There was another young couple with their hands all over each other. The girl's left arm was neatly tucked into the boy's right. They held each other close and kept whispering stuff in each other's ears. With each whisper from the girl, the boy burst out laughing. Same with the girl when the boy told her something. Honeymoon period, John assumed. They looked happy. Their faces were drowned in what looked like a whole lot of love.

"The feeling of being in love," John said, letting out a heavy sigh.

He also saw a table with four friends talking and laughing loudly. They slapped each other on the back, hi-5'd the guy who went up to a girl and asked for her number, looked intently into the screen of one's mobile (probably the profile of some girl), and they were genuinely having fun.

He turned to his side and saw the book beside him. He took it in his hand, brushed his thumb against it, placed it on the table and started to walk out of the cafe.

"Sir! Sir! Your book," a girl called out from behind him.

"No, it's not mine," he replied.

"But I saw you reading it."

"Do you read?" he asked, reentering the cafe. "Yes."

"Consider this my gift to you." "I'll

accept it under one condition"

"What's that?"

"Write down your number on the front page and I'll take this book with me."

"I'm sorry. I don't do dates or relationships. I'm not the kind of guy who likes being around people."

"Yet you're here in the most occupied coffee shop in the city," she shot back.

"I'm here because I like to read and I like their Iced Tea. I'm okay being on my own in a crowd of unknown people. I don't really prefer knowing people. I feel like they're a nuisance sometimes."

"Everyone's a nuisance sometimes."

"Yes. But I don't have the patience or the heart to be around people. I'm more of a 'born alone, die alone' person."

"People can change. You know that, right?"

"I do. I just don't see myself changing after 34 years of living this way. And also, for the sake of clarity, I like this way of life."

"Okay. You can't blame a girl for trying, right? I just thought you looked cute and mysterious."

"I don't know about that. Tell you what? Here's my number. Your effort and courage deserve something," John said and wrote his number on the front page of the book.

"I'm Riya," she announced.

"Hi Riya, I'm John. I know you have my number. But I hope you will understand if I don't respond enthusiastically when you reach out to me. It's not personal; I'm just not a people person."

"You've made that very clear, John. Thank you for the number."

DAre TO DAvID

Once upon a time (actually not so long ago), there was a boy. He fell in love with a girl. She loved him back. And they got married. They moved into a nice flat in the city and furnished it with pretty things. They made each other hopelessly happy. They were both working; they were both earning well—everything was set.

But there was a problem…they hated their jobs. Not the normal frustration with management or the team; it was the deep-seated resentment and red-hot rage fuelled hatred for the company and its people.

They were not like a usual couple. David (the boy) was the gentle, loving, sensitive and sometimes, insecure person who would be hugged into warmth by the assured and confident presence of Kiara (the girl).

By the traditional stereotype of how relationships have been popularised, the boy is the saviour and the girl is in distress, right? It wasn't the case with them. David was the lost boy and Kiara swooped in and saved him from drowning in his own mess.

He didn't have too many friends and the ones he did have mocked the hell out of him for how sensitive he was. The only person who seemed to understand his chaotic insides (other than Kiara) was his best friend, Disha. Until Kiara became his primary protector, it was Disha who held him together when he went through phases of turmoil. Essentially, outside of his single mother, these were the only two people he genuinely cared about.

The strong influence of his mother on his life and her slightly overpowering nature made him a bit too timid for school and college. He spent his entire student life trying to fight his demons and become an outspoken human being, but to no avail. That's where Disha came in. She became his voice and the nudge from behind that pushed him out of his comfort zone. Disha introduced him to Kiara because he said he had a crush on her.

His previous attempts at expressing his feelings to girls didn't go too well. They weren't too appreciative of or attracted by how emotionally available (perceived as vulnerable), expressive, and articulate (perceived as cheesy) he was. But with Kiara, he met someone who appreciated his so-called vulnerability and acknowledged the fact that his sensitivity didn't make him any less masculine than the fairytale heroes people grew up watching.

In fact, after their first date, she sent this text to Disha : "It's so refreshing to see a guy be so open and emotionally honest. Such a sweet, innocent boy, Disha. I like him!"

At present, David is struggling emotionally with a palpable disconnect with the work part of his life. He contemplated quitting every night but didn't know what he would do if he left the job. His quitting would also place the financial responsibility entirely on Kiara's shoulders and he wasn't comfortable with that.

She already has enough on her plate with a hectic job and the responsibility of taking care of his oft-fragile emotions. He also noticed how her patience with him (which had historically been pitch perfect) had started to show quite a few cracks.

"Why is she losing her patience? Does she not know I need her to be patient with me? And she's occupied with work all the time. How will I even share my fears with her? Every time I go to her, it ends in an argument and we fight. I never get to actually tell her what I wish to do. How do I find the right time to discuss this with her?" he wondered.

He rubbed his face with both hands as if the heat from his palms would warm his insides. As he heaved a heavy sigh, his mobile phone rang.

Written on the display was "Disha calling…" He

picked up immediately.

"Look who is calling me? What a surprise!" he said.

"What?! I'm the only one who calls you. Have you ever once called me?"

"Okay…okay…But it has been a long time since you last called me, hence my surprise."

"That's true. But why should I call you?"

"What?! What sort of a question is that?" David hit back.

"You're no longer my responsibility, David. You're Kiara's problem now. I'm free from the shackles that have held me back since college!"

"Oh…I see. I didn't know that's how you saw me. David Shackles. Does make for a good name though, right?"

"I'm kidding, man. How have you been?"

"Ummm…I've been okay, I guess. I wasn't okay last night, but today I am."

"So my phone call today means you're going to be better than okay tomorrow."

"Haha, I hope," David said with a forced smile.

"Tell me, what's going on? What thoughts are you grinding in your jobless brain today?"

What started with a hesitant "ummmm….." ended 25 minutes later when David was done venting his heart out.

"Whoa! It's been a long time since I've heard you go on an uncontrollable emotional rant. And let's just say, I did kind of enjoy it. Not your pain, but the fact that you unloaded all your worries on my front lawn."

"I'm in a fix, Disha. I don't know what to do. I know I want to quit. But I don't know what I will do after I quit. I want to take a break from work. I feel like I'm going to explode if I don't."

"I understand."

"How do I tell her this? She is ALWAYS busy. Emails, phone calls, excel sheets. I feel like I'm living alone."

"Mmm…"

"I feel bad for her, too. Because I know how hectic her job is, but she's letting it consume her. And I feel like I'm becoming collateral damage."

"We all go through phases, David. The two of you are going through something now. But I'm sure she won't discourage you from quitting if that's what you really want."

"We had a conversation a year ago when I said sometimes I feel like quitting my job. At the time, she put her arm around my shoulder and told me she will type my resignation mail for me if that's what I wanted. I know she will support me, but I've not had the time to discuss what my options are. And I can't decide without her."

"Okay. I think it's time now."

"For?"

"For me to drop the bomb."

"What?"

"You need to decide on your own. You can't go pouting to her every time you're confused. Not to her, not to me. Not to anybody. You need to learn to make your own decisions. It is your life. We helped you with your decisions for a long time, but now it's time for you to start making them on your own."

"I can't do something you guys don't approve." "Why

not? Who made us your boss?"

"I don't know. It's not like that. I need your validation when I decide to do something. You know that!"

"I do. And that's what I'm saying. If there is something you want to do that we don't agree with, it's our problem. You should still go ahead and do it. You don't need our approval or our validation."

"Yes. It's very easy, na?"

"It isn't easy. But it's possible"

"Mmm…"

"You're good enough, David. You're smarter than both of us. Do you know that?"

"The two of you keep saying that. I don't believe that for one second."

"In that case, okay. You're dumb as a bag of nuts, David. You don't quit. Stay in your sh*tty company and pull your hair out. Be unhappy and go on with your life."

"Disha…"

"No, I'm saying it without sarcasm. I'm saying if you can't decide this on your own, maybe you shouldn't be doing it."

"But I want to do it."

"And?"

"…"

"Hello? You there?"

"Yes, okay. I'll talk to her and do it."

"I'm going to have to give you a deadline." "Okay."

"Tomorrow EOD. 6PM."

"Are you mad? How will I find a suitable time from now to then? She is so caught up with work!"

"I don't know. 6PM tomorrow. Bye."

"Wait wait wait!"

"What?" "Thank

you" "For what?"

"For today."

"Honestly, your answer should've been 'for the last 10 years of my life', but okay. Sure. You're welcome."

"I don't know how, but whenever I feel lost in thought or I'm on the verge of being overwhelmed by something, you text or call me. I don't know. It's comforting. Makes me feel like I'm not alone."

"David. My overthinking 27-year-old baby, you're not alone. You're never alone."

"Yes. I'm not."

"And just so you know, if you feel alone because Kiara's not available, you can always call me. I'll gladly get you out of your mental mess. In fact, I taught her how to do it, so I'm the expert."

"You may regret making this offer."

"I didn't know I had to offer. I thought you knew it already. But okay, I guess people forget friends after they get married."

"Just because I don't call you, does not mean I don't remember you."

"Sure, David. Whatever helps you sleep at night!" "Disha."

"What?"

"Thank you."

"Okay, David. You're welcome. I love you. Go have dinner now. Don't burn your brain to death!"

"Love you too."

A little while later, his phone pinged with a message:

Okay, listen to me. Don't worry too much. Everything will fall in place exactly the way it's supposed to. Do what you feel is right. You will always find a way, with or without anybody else's support.

Also, it's nice to be needed by you once in a while. Hasn't happened much for years. And as much as I want you not to be dependent on anyone, I wouldn't mind a little dependency on me once in a while.

Makes me feel useful, you know?

It's like my validation. If you think I gave you validation whenever you needed, please know you gave me as much validation as I gave you. That's how humans work. And not that you don't know, I have all the love in the world for you. And I hope to always be there for both - the good and the bad. Just go tell her and resign. Take a break and find what you wish to do. But remember, being at home without a job is going to be challenging. You will feel useless sometimes, your confidence will reach very low points. Be prepared for it. Always remember why you chose to leave that job. Remind yourself that money isn't more important than your mental peace.

David smiled.

"Thank you, Disha. And you gave me the perfect way to tell her. A letter!" he thought.

He hit send and took a pen and paper in his hands.

Kiara,

I've been fighting something within me for the longest time, but I could never bring myself to you with it. You've been so busy with work that every time I tried to bring it up, we ended up in an argument even before I could tell you about it. I don't know if I'm being too much of a baby with my emotions or you're losing patience with me. But whatever it is, I don't like it. But that's okay, we can figure it out later. This is the first time I'm writing you a letter since I proposed to you with one. Last time I put pen and paper together, I knew it would make you happy. This time, I'm not too sure.

I want to resign from my company. I get nightmares about work. When you're sound asleep after a tiring day at work, I wake up sweating. I go to the restroom at the office and cry sometimes. I don't know what I want to do going forward, but I know what I don't want to do. And that's this job.

This decision will force you to bear the brunt of our financial commitments, but I promise not to be too much of a burden. I will find something I want to do really soon and be out of your hair.

I'm terrified of how you will react to this decision of mine and I don't know if you think it's the right thing to do. But I do know that I need to do this. I'm not sure if I'm being reasonable here, because I'm making a unilateral decision for myself knowing full well that it impacts both of us. It may be too much to ask, but can you find a way to understand why I need to do this? And can you also find a way to be okay with me for doing this? Can you please forgive me if I'm being selfish?

I'm really sorry for what this decision will do to you.

I will leave this letter for you. Please read it whenever you're free. If you read it and find that you need time to have a conversation with me about this, you can take all the time you need. I will not ask you if you read the letter, I will not ask you if you are okay with it, I will not even bring up this topic. I will give you all the space you deserve.

In all the years we've been together, I've never once felt good enough for you. But every time you stroked my hair and said you were lucky to have me, I would heave a sigh of relief.

Now, more than ever, I need that sigh.

I know I'm a handful to deal with. I know I'm difficult to manage when I'm not in the right space. I'm sorry for being a burden and I'm sorry for being something for you to 'take care of'. Disha told me something today that made me think that I need to start being my own person. I will try and become more assured of myself. I will try not to need you all the time to feel secure. I don't know how, but I'll find a way. Okay? I promise.

Before that, if you feel like I'm too much to handle, it's okay if you lose patience with me. You don't have to feel the need to protect me. If you don't lose patience with me, who will?

Lots and lots and lots and lots of love,

Your neurotic husband,

D.

He placed the letter on her pillow and went to sleep. Kiara reached home late that night and saw the envelope. She read it and looked at David with the letter still in her hand. She ran her left hand through his hair.

"Hey," he said with his voice shaking.

She placed the letter on the bedside table and snuggled into the comforter.

"It's okay," she said.

"Really?" David's eyes widened. "Yes."

Before David could hug her, Kiara rolled him from his side to his back, lay on his chest and put her arms around him.

"I love taking care of you. You're not a burden to me. At all. Ever."

David was silent.

"You're going to cry, aren't you?" Kiara said, smiling.

David's silence continued.

"Oh you're already crying then," she said, still with her face on his chest.

A couple of tears flowed down his face and onto her hair.

"I'm sorry."

"Please, Kiara. I'm sorry. You have nothing to be sorry for."

She sat up, took his head and put it on her lap.

She ran her hand through his hair and said, "I'm really lucky to have you, David. You're the best thing that ever happened to me."

A tear made its way out of her eye and onto his forehead.

"If I didn't have you, I wouldn't be half the person I am. I want you to know that," she said.

"Me too."

"I'll take off work tomorrow." "Why?"

"I have a resignation mail to type." David

laughed.

"That, you do."

D_{IA}ry O_f A CeO

27-June-2023

It's been 10 years since I took over as CEO of this company. In that time, I've taken countless flights, flown millions of miles, met thousands of minds, given umpteen interviewers, written for the most prestigious business magazines and tabloids, and created a network of high net worth individuals that would evoke a bit of envy in even the most secure of individuals.

I travel 15-20 days a month, which means I'm in a hotel room more often than I'm home. I wake up to an unoccupied pillow more often than my wife's face. I spend more time watching the news than my son's life. I talk more on Microsoft Teams than I do to my daughter. Both of them are in college now and they barely know me. Sometimes, I feel guilty about calling myself their father. By designation, I probably am. But in reality, they don't have a father; they've never had one. My wife tries to be both, but how much can one person do? On nights like those, I question if any of this is worth it. What's the point of being so successful if I can't share it with people I love?

But no, there's another side to this. All this success gives me recognition, makes me feel good about myself, satisfies my ambition, and earns me money—oney that will allow my son and daughter to do what they choose to do. Money that will keep my wife comfortable. Money that will secure my family's future. Money that gives me and my family access to special places.

What should I do?

I know my company's revenue and profit performance for every year since 2000. But I can't remember my son's birthday. I know my project team loves using pastel colours in our office space because it calms people down, but I don't know what colour my daughter loves, or when she needs calming, or how she can be calmed.

Everywhere I go, people surround me. They give me everything I need, everything I want, and then some. People wait in line to talk to me. But, when I'm home, my kids can't bring themselves to say anything more than a "Hi" or "Bye". Nor do I! I can make speeches in front of the whole world, build conversations with people I've never met, but I can't talk to my children. I don't know what to say. I'm left speechless every single time.

They spend hours telling my wife stories about their friends in college, but they won't so much as sit with me in the same room for more than 15 minutes without her. I feel important everywhere except my home. I feel loved and respected by everyone, except my children. I feel comfortable in the hustle and bustle of corporate meetings, but I'm terrified of the silence in my living room. The whole world lets me be an insider, but I feel like an outsider when I'm inside my own home.

What should I do? Continue to be the country's most admired CEO? Or be my wife's only husband and my kids' only father?

DIAry Of The mInDleSS GenIuS

Hi. I'm Rahul.

I'm smarter than 99.998% of the people in the world. At least, that's what my IQ tests say. I'm 24 years old and work as a developer in the world's largest tech company. I earn more money than I'll ever need, and I live alone in a flat large enough for a family of 10.

I've always known I was intelligent. But, I was also always told what to do, when to do and how to go about doing it. Despite being sharper than everyone around me, I never once thought of asking them why I had to do any of it. My father, may God bless him, loved engineering. Most of his friends had shifted base to foreign land and made something of themselves with their engineering background. But no, not just any engineering; they were all computer science graduates. So, in his eyes, all other branches were pointless. Computer Science was the Big Boss.

He signed me up for abacus when I was 6 years old & programming when I was 11. It is said that 8,900+ programming languages have been created by humans over the years, but very few of those fall under the 'most used' bucket. But will you believe me if I tell you I have learned 122 programming languages? I learned 70 of those even before getting to college. The thing about programming is that it's all about logic. Any problem can be solved in any programming language but the logic will remain the same in all of them. Only the syntax varies. It's like a book written in 50 languages. The content is the same, but the words aren't.

Anyway, I was told to dive headfirst into the Ocean of code and I did. I've been swimming there ever since. I created multiple web applications while in college, some of which my father was able to sell to firms.

In the final year of my engineering, I created something that had a brain of its own. Something that knew everything and could instantly access that information to solve anything and everything. That's how my company picked me up. They purchased my web application and offered me a job.

My father didn't want me to run a business. He jumped at the opportunity. After a year in the India office, I was asked to move to their headquarters. Before I could think and decide, my father agreed to it—packed and shipped me off to Silicon City.

I've been in this company for 3 years now, and I've been promoted thrice. But I see people around me and feel like I don't belong here. They have a burning passion for what they do. They look so happy when they create something. They are constantly fishing for new challenges because they feel so connected to what they're doing. I work with them and I achieve similar things, and maybe do even more than they do, but I feel absolutely nothing. I don't go out looking for new challenges. There's no sense of pride, achievement, or connection.

I do what I'm asked to do and get back home when I'm done for the day.

The other day, a group of colleagues were having coffee and I heard one of them say, "This job is my calling". In a matter of seconds, the rest of them were all being vocal about how they felt the same.

I've been part of discussions where I could feel people's passion fly across the room. However, I have never felt that way. I know a lot of things, and one of those things happens to be the knowledge that I don't belong here.

Coding is not my calling.

I was thrust into the world of programming by my father. I didn't ask why. I didn't say no. I didn't think. I did whatever he wanted me to do.

Looking back, it feels like I hardly used my brain for anything other than coding. I feel like I could've asked a few more questions. Tried a few more things. Maybe I would've been able to figure out where my interest lay.

If I'm this good at something I don't even like, how good will I be at something I love? I guess we'll never know.

Isn't it amazing how the smartest minds can be turned into machines that don't think for themselves and just do what they're programmed to do? Yes, maybe I can design a solution to literally everything the world needs. But my question is, how am I any different from the programmes I create? The programme is the brain, the computer is the machine.

I'm the brain, my body is the machine. I just don't see the difference.

DISTAnCe mAkeS The heArT GrOw fOnDer

" Dad, tell me about mom!" she said one day.

"What, honey?" I asked.

"Tell me about mom. I don't remember much about her and all my friends keep talking about their moms. I don't know anything about mine."

I look at her, standing there with expectant eyes. We had lost her mother–my wife–when she was young. It's no surprise that she doesn't remember much about her mom. So I decided to indulge in her request.

"Okay, sit with me."

My little girl came and sat on my lap. "Tell

me. What do you want to know?"

"What was mom like?" She asked, curiosity and longing burning in her eyes.

"She was the most amazing woman I ever met." "How

did you meet her?"

"She was my best friend's girlfriend's best friend," I said, with a small smile on my face as I remembered the good old days.

"Okay, tell me more."

"The four of us used to hang out together all the time. In the process of spending all that time in each other's presence, we ended up falling in love with each other."

"Okay, who said it first?"

"Who do you think?"

"You!"

"That's right. I did."

"Did she say it back immediately?"

"Oh no, she didn't. I had to wait months for her to actually tell me she loved me."

"Why?"

I shrugged. "Her version of the story is that she didn't want to say it until she felt it in full force within her."

"What's your version?"

"That your mom loved letting me beg her for those 3 words. She was a cunning little creature, not unlike you."

"Do you miss her?" "Every

day."

"What do you do when you miss her?"

"I look at you because you are the spitting image of your mother. You're the 12-year-old version of her."

Her face brightened hearing that, glad to have found something in common with her late mother. "Really? Do I really look like her?"

"Yes, exactly like her and I love you just like I loved her."

"I love you too, dad."

I kissed her on the forehead and stroked her hair. "What did

you like most about her?"

"You're not done with your questions?"

"Not at all. I have a lot more."

I sighed in resignation. This will go on for a while. "I

will repeat. What did you like most about her?"

"Whenever I had a bad day and I came home, I just instantly felt better. Her mere presence would make me forget my worries."

"I don't understand."

"When you're sad, what do you do?" "I

come to you."

"Exactly. I went to your mom"

"Ohhh…"

"Yes. She was my guardian angel."

I could see the question in her eyes before they came out. "Was mom ever scared?"

"Why do you ask that?"

"I'm scared often. So, if I'm like mom, she must have also felt very scared."

"Yes, your mom was definitely scared of a lot of things."

"What did she do when she was scared of something?" "She

would hug me."

"I do that! I really am like her!" Her eyes lit up. "Yes,

does that help you?"

"Yes, dad."

"Good, I'm glad." "Do

you get scared?"

"Good question, sweetheart. Good question. Yes, I do."

"Who helps you when you're scared?" "It

used to be your mom."

"And now?"

"You."

"How? I don't even know when you're scared. How could I help you?"

"You need not know it. But when I'm scared, I sit with you and ask you to massage my head."

"You did that last week! Were you afraid of something?" "I

was not afraid. I was just a tiny bit sad."

"Why?"

"Because I was missing your mother. It was her birthday."

"Oh…"

There was silence for a while.

"What is your favourite memory of mom?" she continued.

"The day she delivered you, I entered the hospital room; she turned to me and said, 'Don't you dare love her more than you love me'. Then, she handed you to me. That is my all-time favourite memory of her."

"So…" "So

what?"

"Do you love me more than you love her?" "I

love you both equally, sweetheart."

"No! You can choose only one. Who do you love more
- mom or me?"

"Will you be mad if I say I love your mom more?" "I

don't know."

"I'm probably gonna sound like a horrible dad right now,
but I think I love your mom more."

"That's okay, dad."

"Really? It's okay?"

"Yes! I know you love me, so it's okay if you love mom
more."

"For a child, you're incredibly mature. Do you know that?"

"Was mom mature, too?"

"Oh! You have no idea."

"How am I like her when I've not spent any time with
her? I'm always with you, so I should be more like you,
right?"

"First of all, what you are is 50% of me and 50% of your
mother. So, even if she's not here with you, she is within
you. So you will always carry her characteristics. Also,
your mother was a far better person than I can ever be.
So, everything I teach you is what I want you to be, which
is a kind and gentle soul like your mother.

And so far, you're exactly that. I'm so proud of what you're becoming."

"Thank you, dad."

"Can you love someone even after they are gone?" she continued.

"Yes. Sometimes, you love them even more after they're gone."

"But how? You can't see or talk to them. How will love grow?"

"You can remember them. Feel the things they left behind with you. And that's enough for love to grow."

"I remember this dialogue from a film. Distance makes the heart grow fonder. What you're saying…is it similar?"

I couldn't help myself. I laughed out loud.

"Why are you laughing, dad? Tell me!" she asked, smacking my bicep.

I continued laughing, and she continued slapping my hand. A few seconds later, a couple of tears found their way down my face.

"Why are you crying, dad?" "I'm

not crying, honey." "There are

tears on your face."

"What you said about distance and the heart…it was the last thing your mother ever said to me. Just before she passed away, she held my hand and told me distance makes the heart grow fonder. So, when you said that, I couldn't help laughing. These tears? They're tears of joy.

"Because you don't just look like your mother, you think like her and you talk like her. And that makes me the happiest man alive."

TAXI

hO1A OuTSTATIOn

TN01AN9507
Driver Name : Raju
Vehicle model : Mahindra Verito (Green) Your
ride has arrived.

Vijay walked through the parking lot towards the pin location looking for his ride home. He was returning home for the 5th time in 6 months. He located the vehicle and put his bags in the backseat.

"Anna, can you please turn on the AC?" he requested, as he adjusted the passenger's seat and locked himself with the seat belt.

"Sure," said Raju.

"How long have you been in Chennai?"

"Just a year."

"You're here with your family?"

"No, I don't have that luxury. My wife and daughter are in Thenkaasi"

"Where do you stay?"

"In my car." "Really?"

"Yes. Helps me save money on rent. I can get my daughter something she likes when I go home."

"How often do you go home?"

"Pongal. My daughter's birthday, in June. Diwali."

"You don't miss them?"

"I do. But I need to find ways of feeding them." "If

you sleep in your car, where do you bathe?"

"In the bus depot; there's a corner where drivers can go and take a bath. There's no washroom or anything, just a water outlet. You can carry your own bucket and soap and take a shower there."

"And you're okay with this life?"

"I am. I get to give my family a life through this." "You

own the car, right?"

"Yes."

"How many years remain in the loan term?" "I

have just 6 more months. Then I'm free."

"So you will get to save more. Maybe you can afford to stay in a decent place."

"Maybe. But I'll try and keep things this way. Save a bit more so I can go home more often. Spent a little more time with my family."

"If you don't mind me asking, what is your income?"

"I make roughly 50,000/- every month. But after fuel expenses, EMI & my food, I have about 10,000/- in my hand."

"That's not too bad, right?"

"Not bad at all. Some people call me on long trips; I get to stay for 2 or 3 days with them. That really helps. I get 5,000/- for each of those trips outside of the fuel expense. So I have started reaching out to more people and letting them know I'm open to it. In the past few months, I've done 8 long trips. So I was able to buy a earring for my daughter."

"Oh, that's so great." "Thank

you, sir."

"Here, take this left, the road is better."

"Sure."

You have arrived at your location.

"It was a great ride, anna. Thank you."

"Thanks sir. I enjoyed talking to you."

Vijay paid an additional 500/- to the driver. "Please have a briyani with as many leg pieces as you want. My treat."

"Oh no. Please, this is too much. I can't accept this."

"Had I not come home today, I would've spent this money on my lunch and dinner. So don't worry. You can have a very good meal."

"Thank you so much, sir!" Raju beamed.

Vijay exchanged numbers, in case he ever needed a driver to go on a trip.

A few months later, Raju received a call. "Briyani

Vijay sir" was the name on his screen.

"Sirr! How are you?" Raju's smile could be felt on the other side of the phone call.

"I'm fine, anna. Are you free this weekend from Friday to Sunday?"

"Yes, I am. Tell me, sir."

"My parents and I are planning on going someplace. Can you drive us?"

"Sure, sir. Where do you want to go?"

"Thenkaasi"

"Sir?"

"Thenkaasi, Raju anna. Will you show us around your hometown? Be a tour guide"

"Sir, forget 3 days. I'll show you around for 3 weeks. I'll come to your place on Friday morning."

"Yes. I'll share my location with you." "You don't need to, sir. I remember" "Seriously? You dropped me months ago!" "Yes sir. But you bought me briyani."

pArenTS-In-1One

“ “Vaniii! Let’s have lunch!”

“Coming, Meera amma,” replied the 23-year-old before rushing towards the dining room.

When she got to the dining table, Mithran’s mouth was already filled with food.

“Sorry, ma. I couldn’t wait. I was famished,” he said, an apologetic smile on his face.

“Ayyo, please have it, Appa. How does it taste?” “A+!”

Meera smiled at the compliment before beckoning Vani to eat. “Come Vani, here’s your plate.”

Meera and Mithran were an old couple in their 60’s who stayed alone in a villa. Their sons, Krish & Arjun, had settled in the UK and couldn’t visit more than once a year. They video-called every evening to check on their parents, but that was the extent to which they could engage with them.

Work, kids, friends—there was too much going on in their lives away from home. Both sons tried regularly to get their stubborn parents to shift base to the UK, but to no avail. It's like they say; no son has ever won an argument against his father and no daughter, against her mom, right?

Vani was the caretaker of this kind old couple. She grew up in a children's home closeby and was still staying there helping out with the kids. She joined as a caretaker at 20 years of age and had stayed with them for 3 years. The three of them had developed a very close bond. Meera and Vani spent time in the kitchen trying out new recipes for Mithran to taste. Mithran, on the other hand, made a list of movies that the three of them could watch while they had their meals.

After lunch, Mithran called Vani to the living room. "Foot massage, appa?"

"No, my dear. I want to talk to you about something." "What is it about?"

"Remember Ramya, my old business partner's daughter?"

"Yes, I met her a few weeks ago when you were at a Rotary meeting."

"Yes. She really likes you. She called to ask me if you would join her as her personal assistant."

"Oh…"

"What do you think?" he said, stroking her hair.

"I don't know anything about how an office works. What will I do there?"

"You will take care of things that go through her. Just like you do here. And she's a lovely girl. You can learn a lot from her. It will help you build a career for yourself."

Vani remained silent.

"You aren't thinking of being a caretaker for the rest of your life, are you?"

"I love doing this. It is personal. It is fulfilling. What's wrong with this?" Vani asked, slapping his legs.

Meera walked in and sat beside her.

"But you're a smart girl, Vani. You need to try something that gives you the opportunity to make something of yourself."

Vani didn't seem convinced.

"Okay, Vani. I was going to save it for later, but now seems like a good time to let you know."

"Let me know what?"

"Meera and I are thinking of leaving for the UK." "Oh on

a trip? For how many days?"

"No, we're planning to leave permanently." Vani

turned and looked at Meera.

Meera leaned in and kissed her forehead.

"We are looking to leave in the next 6–12 months.

We want to help you find a good job before we go," Mithran continued.

"I don't know what to say," Vani said.

"Ramya is starting a new business division. If you join now, you will be able to learn how the business works from scratch. You can grow along with the company. You take a day or two. Think about it."

She nodded.

~

The following morning, as Vani was placing ironed clothes in Meera's cupboard, Mithran walked in.

"So?"

"I don't want to go before you leave. I'll join her after you go to the UK," she said.

"No, Vani. She needs someone now, it'll be good for you."

"I'll find another job, then. I won't leave before you two leave."

"Meera! Ask Arjun to book our tickets for next week. Vani wants us to leave."

"Appa!!!" she slammed the cupboard's door shut.

"Vani, I'm older than you. If you want to play hard, I have no problem in doing so."

"Why are you so eager to chase me away?"

"Because when opportunities knock on our door, we ought to take them."

"Mmm." She walked to the kitchen.

Mithran followed her.

"This girl is very irritating."

"So are you!" she shot back.

~

A few hours later, as she served them lunch, Vani said, "Okay, I'll go."

"Really?" Meera looked at her.

"Yes. But I will come here every weekend to be with you. So whoever you appoint to replace me can't be here on Saturdays and Sundays."

"We aren't going to have anyone. So you are more than welcome," Mithran declared.

"Why not?"

"Because I'm not sick anymore. Meera and I can manage on our own until we go."

Later that night, as Mithran turned off the TV and walked into the bedroom, Meera was sitting up.

"Were you waiting for me?" he asked.

"Yes."

"Am I in trouble?" he laughed.

"When did you decide to leave for the UK?" "I

didn't. I just wanted to give her the push."

"What if she figures it out and wants to come back? What if she quits that job?"

"She won't."

"How do you know?" "I

don't know. I hope."

He lay down and turned off the lights.

After a few minutes of silence, Meera tapped on his shoulder.

"Mm?"

"It's not the worst idea, you know?"

"Lying to Vani? Yes. I know!"

"No. Not that. I meant us moving to the UK." "You

want to move?"

"It's been 10 years since we've stayed together as a family. Now we have grandkids there and we're sitting here. Don't you want to be with them?" She asked, puzzled.

"I didn't realise you missed them so much."

"Of course, I do. They're my sons. My granddaughters. I want to stay with them. Help them grow. Watch them play."

"Mmm…"

"Don't you feel lonely?"

"I don't feel lonely when you're around." Meera

moved closer and lay on his chest.

"I love you for that. But I want us to leave this world with no regrets."

"And you're afraid we will regret not spending more time with them if we continue to live here." It wasn't a question because he could guess his wife's thoughts.

She hugged him tighter, nodding in agreement. Mithran felt a tear touch his skin through his vest.

"I know it's been a long time since our sons moved out, but that was the life we helped them choose, right? We gave them the option of staying here with the business. They chose something different. That's why we sold our business too."

"I know. But I miss them. Every night, I walk to their rooms and wish them good night even though they aren't here. There isn't a day I don't wish they had chosen differently."

"Okay, I'll talk to them about the Visa."

"Really?"

He kissed her on the forehead. "Yes."

"You don't mind going there?"

"Why will I mind living with my sons?"

"You go out here; you have friends in the rotary club. You have old business acquaintances. You will have nobody there."

"The only reason I need the club or my other business friends is because they're not here. If I have them at home, I won't need any of this."

"Are you sure? I know I will be fully satisfied being home with them. But I want you to be absolutely certain before we decide to go."

"I am certain, Meera. You're right; we must have chosen to go sooner."

"No. This is good; we can plan our goodbyes here."

"There's only one goodbye you care about."

"Yes. I want to buy her something."

"We'll go out tomorrow," Mithran promised.

The next morning, they went shopping for Vani. They bought her a laptop, a new pair of clothes to wear on her first day at office, and sandals.

When they presented her with it, a tear found its way down Vani's cheeks.

She hugged them both.

"I'm going to visit you every week; I promise," she said.

"We know you will."

Vani left for her new job the following week.

~

"5," Mithran said.

"What 5?" Meera asked, confused.

"That's the number of days we haven't seen Meera in the past 3 years."

"Mmm…"

"The house feels haunted, doesn't it?"

"Yes. Exactly like the day Arjun left, two years after Krish."

"This isn't going to be easy." "No,"

Meera agreed.

"She'll be here this weekend; I guess that's something to look forward to," she added.

"Today's Tuesday. How are you going to pass the next 3 days?" Mithran snapped.

"Don't be a baby. Find enough movies for us to get to the weekend!" she ordered.

"This will be our new life now."

"Not for long. We'll be playing with our grandkids next year."

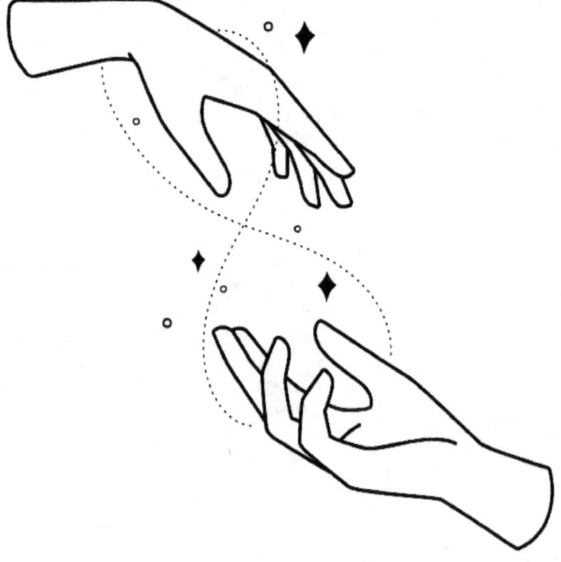

Sai Tharun

reverSe-VAllDATIOn

There's a guy who is nice to everyone.

A guy who is liked by everyone. A guy who never loses patience with anyone around him.
He's kind to his family, his friends, the waiter at the restaurant, the credit card lady who is calling him for the hundredth time. He is kind to every single person—strangers and known faces alike.

Everyone praises him. His patience extends beyond friendly small-talk; he is the go-to person for his friends when they're feeling lost or lonely. He listens patiently to all their problems, offers solutions if asked and lets them vent. He sends good morning texts at the beginning of every week to his closest friends to help them tame their Monday blues.

He forgives them for their mistakes; doesn't judge them for their past actions but holds them responsible for their present and future ones. He ensures he's present in their lives so they know they have someone in their corner.

Sounds like the perfect guy, right?

But it also sounds a little too good to be true, does it not?

Is it even humanly possible for someone to be nice to everyone in their life? Even a machine is defective in a batch of several thousand. So in the multiple relationships that we juggle between, as humans, we are bound to have one or two that buck the trend.

There will be a relationship that brings out qualities in us that others can't imagine we embody. So, this guy I'm talking about, if you have a guy or a girl in your life like this, I've found a name for them. I call them the reverse-validators.

Why? I'll start with a very wise quote from a very wise TV character Joey Tribbiani.

"In this world, there is no such thing as an unselfish good deed."

Taking the discussion forward with this legendary quote, I would like to say that there is a reason he is kind and patient with everyone around him. There is a reason he goes around voluntarily listening to people's problems. That reason? He needs that to survive.

Every time someone comes to him upset and leaves feeling better, his ego gets a boost. And if his ego gets a boost, he feels better about himself. He feels useful. He feels like there's some purpose to his life.

Now the most logical follow-up question is why does he need that ego boost, right?

That's because he is lonely. He's been solving others' problems his entire life that nobody has ever asked him how he's doing. Nobody ever checks on him. Nobody ever calls him just for the sake of it. Everybody assumes his life is perfect, and that's the reason he is able to be so good with those around him.

This false narrative that, frankly, he helped build is now the reason he is stuck without any real emotional support. Since others assume he has it all figured out and his ego is now too inflated to go out and ask for help, he resorts to something he is used to. What's that? Being nice and kind to people. He helps people, listens to them, stays with them when they need him, helps them feel better about themselves and gives them the validation they need.

Now, this has an additional effect. Every time they leave feeling happier than they were when they came to him, his life suddenly finds meaning. His life finds a purpose. His action is validated. His ego is preserved. His self-image is preserved. But make no mistake. The person helping someone in need? He needs that someone as much as that someone needs him. His way of finding validation is giving that validation to someone else.

Emotional loneliness can do that to you. When you're used to a certain way of life, you tend to stick to it. So if you're used to taking help, you will always take help. If you're used to never taking help, you will always hesitate to take help. So, you will find alternate routes to your destination. And that destination is common for all of us: validation.

It's easier to feel validated when we have people with us. So instead of waiting for others to come to them and share validation, they go in search of them. They find these people, give them validation and find their own, in the process.

But I'm not complaining here. There are worse ways to live. And frankly, even though this may not be entirely healthy from a psychological standpoint, I have to say this is an amazing way to make the world a better place. But it sure isn't ideal for the long-term because once these sources of validation reduce and the intensity starts fading, the emptiness settles in, and it may not be easy to chase away.

Once they reach that point, the reverse-validators will wish they had someone like them in their own lives; to give them validation and also take some in return. Because reverse-validators never take without giving; nor can they give without taking. It's a package deal. Some would argue it's a pretty good package deal, but I'm still on the fence for this one.

Concept note : Reverse-validation and its relation with emotional loneliness. Patent pending.

Author : Shyam Date

: 12-04-2023

SOulInG AwAy

I remember a wave of pain sharply shooting up my chest. I remember trying, unsuccessfully, to move my left arm. And then it all went blank. Now I'm floating in the air. Is this what I think it is? Have I finally been served with my eviction notice from Earth?

But if I'm dead, I must be able to see what's happening back in the old age home where my life reached its inevitable end. What are they doing? How long has it been since I moved on? How do I figure out any of this?

What's this blue button? Well, blue is my favourite colour. I mean, was. Actually, it is. I'm still there, right? Maybe not on earth, but somewhere. So, yes. I'm going to push this blue button, hoping my favourite colour brings some clarity to my currently blurred picture.

Whoosh!

What's happening? Why am I dropping so fast? Oh, I feel nauseous. Blue button is now giving me the blues. Ohhhhh, pressing it was a bad idea. Why am I not slowing down? Where am I falling? This is not making any sense. Is the button going to bring me back to life?

I don't want to live any longer. I have nobody, I was dragged and dropped in an old age home by my only son because he didn't want to take care of me. All my friends are long gone. My lovely wife was taken away by cancer 5 years ago. What do I have to live for? What do I have to look forward to? I see no purpose in life. Please don't send me back to my life on earth, oh God.

Thud

Ouch!

That hurt. This is going to leave a bruise. Where am I? What building is this? Oh wait, I recognise the apartment on the other side of the road. This is my old age home. We're not allowed to be on the terrace, right? That's why I've never been here. So, if I'm here, it definitely means I'm not alive. I'm still dead.

Whoo! What a relief!

Let's go down and see what my old friends are doing. Not sure how long I've been gone, so I'll have to look for the calendar. Does the Home even have a calendar? Why don't I remember all these little details? Was I that lost when I was there? I spent more than 4 years in that place, for crying out loud.

Oh, there's the calendar. It's 2nd July…What was the last date I remember? I was definitely there on 30th June, so I died either on the 30th of June or the 1st of July. Maybe even in the early hours of 2nd July. So it hasn't been that long then. Why is everyone gathered around the office? Let me go check out what's happening there.

"I contacted the son; he says he won't make it. He is going to transfer the money for us to conduct the funeral"

That's Pavithran, the manager of the old age home, saying my son isn't going to do the final rites. Surprise, surprise, eh?

I hear a few of my fellow inmates cursing my son.

I knew my son didn't really love me, but to not even want to see me for the last time, I'm not sure how to feel about that. I had a friend whose daughter cried for days after her boss passed away suddenly. She had worked with her for less than 8 weeks, so when we asked her why she was so upset, she said she never got to thank her manager for everything she taught her. In 8 weeks. Maybe I wasn't the world's greatest dad, but I must have taught him something over the 20-something-years we lived together, right? Did it mean nothing to him?

"Screw his son. We're here. We shall do his last rites and send his soul to rest in peace."

That was Raj, my neighbour. We spent a lot of nights sharing stories with each other. We got along really well and I'm not surprised to see him curse my son out.

"Let's all gather around his bed and share memories of him. Let's send him off properly," said Udhay.

"The funeral is set for tomorrow morning," Pavithran announced.

"So let's do the ceremony here, right after the burial," Kumar added.

"What ceremony?"

"The one where we share memories of Maaran." "Sure."

Okay, so I'm not going to have an empty funeral, after all. Not bad, Maaraa. Not bad.

These guys will all go to sleep now, what should I do? Do I need sleep, now that I'm just a ghost? Okay…let me try to sleep.

~

"It's time to leave! Everyone, please get going!"

That was Pavithran's voice. I actually did end up sleeping. Aahh, I'm feeling good today. Especially considering the fact that it's my funeral.

It's weirdly funny. I'm here and I can see them place my body in the ground and cover it with mud. Oh, people are shedding tears. I didn't realise some of these people cared for me. I guess they just have a good heart.

They're all making their way back to the Home now and I'm floating over them. Imagine if any of them could see me? They would freak the hell out. Aaahhh, that would be so much fun. It's a pity I can't scare these guys. On second thought though, it might induce a heart attack and kill them. So maybe it's better this way.

"Gather around, people!"

"I'll go last," said Raj.

"I'll go first then," said Udhay.

"Sure."

"I will remember Maaran anna as someone who knew how to move on. On my first night here, I couldn't sleep. I was crying uncontrollably when everyone else was already sleeping. He walked up to me and stayed with me the whole night. He let me cry, listened to me, and then sat next to me as I fell asleep. The next morning, he started joking around trying to make me laugh. He joked about reality and how cruel it had been to us.

"Then over the next few weeks, he managed to convince me I'm better off here than with my family. That it was somehow their loss that I'm not with them. I don't know how he did that, but I will never forget how free I've felt since that day and I will never forget what he did for me," Udhay said and wiped the tears off his face.

"He did something similar to me, too. He forced me to smile and wish him good morning everyday. One day, he didn't have to force me. The smile and morning wish came out of me uninvited."

"Yes. He loved smiles. I remember he gave me some sort of dental equipment that holds the mouth open and asked me to place it in my mouth if I felt a frown creep up my face. He had a weird way of getting people to smile."

"And his water trick! If you're crying, don't lie down. Don't cover your face. Leave it open. Drink a glass of water and sit up straight. Or even better, walk. Go get some fresh air and the tears will fall away faster than the hair on your head!"

"I've heard that so many times. I used to hate him for saying that, but I hate to admit that it worked most of the time. I never told him that…maybe I should have. Maybe I should've let him know his ideas made me feel better about myself."

"He really mastered moving on, eh? He had all the answers."

"All of you have already said everything that needs to be known about the man. But there are a few things you need to know," Raj started.

"Most of you came here after Maaran. But I was here before him. The first few weeks, I never saw him cry. He smiled and smiled and smiled so much; it annoyed me. I asked him why and how he could spend the whole day smiling. He told me to wait. I didn't understand what he meant. He told me everyday, "wait, Raj brother. Be patient. When the time comes, I'll let you know". I was confused; does he not know why he's smiling? What do I need to wait for?

"Exactly 4 weeks later, he woke me up in the middle of the night, that mad fellow. He told me this was the reason he smiled everyday.

"'What? To break my sleep?' I had asked him. And his reply was: 'No Raj brother, tonight, when I closed my eyes, I didn't have to hold back tears. I was actually okay." He beamed. And even though I had seen him smile every day since he was here, I felt different. It felt like the smile was something else.

"'So you mean you were faking your smile all these days?' I had asked him and he immediately replied with,'Of course. Fake it till you make it!' raising his hands in victory like he had just won the World Cup.

"The reason he was able to help so many of us was because he knew we needed time. But he also knew that we had to keep our head up during that phase. So he did everything he could to help us hold our heads up. He didn't want us to lay down and become prey to all the nasty thoughts in our head. And God knows we have them.

"Maaraa, rest in peace. Wherever you are, I hope your smile is as wide as it was here when you were with us," Raj said as he sat down on my bed. He gently tapped the bed a few times, as if my body was still there and he was trying to wake me up.

I see a lot of people now with tears lining their eyes. I feel a few in my own, too. All I ever wanted was to leave behind a few good reasons to be missed. Listening to these wonderful old men and women, I feel like I did leave something behind.

I feel like my presence will be missed. Maybe not by my son or my family at home, but by my new family at the Home. I guess I did okay then.

T_{he} O_{ld} m_{An}

Rangasamy walked home from a deserted temple on a quiet morning after performing the rituals on the 10th anniversary of his wife's demise.
They didn't have a family of their own; all they had was each other. They lived in a small 250 sq ft. house with a thatched roof and a washroom on its backside. In the decade that followed his wife's rather sudden death, Ranga had quit drinking.

In 35 years of married life, only one thing ever led to a fight between the two of them: Alcohol. He didn't listen to her; he chugged down 250ml of Rum from the local liquor store every evening on the way home. Now, he crosses that store every evening but refuses to walk in.

The two of them led a modest life. Ranga was a security guard at a boys' school a kilometre from his home and his wife, Lakshmi, was a househelp to a reasonably well-settled family. They tried to have kids, but it was the one thing that eluded them. With just two mouths to feed, their income was never a concern.

Ranga would often fill the void of not having a kid of his own by showering affection on the kids at school. There was one in particular, a 14-year-old named Raghu. He joined the school in Kindergarten and was now in the 9th grade. Every morning, as he entered school, he screamed, "Vanakkam Ranga Thatha".

Ranga met Raghu for the first time a week after his wife passed away. He was upset. Raghu walked up to him during the morning break and asked him why he looked dull. Ranga didn't answer, but Raghu was persistent.

"I'm not well," he replied, looking at the little boy who refused to leave.

"Ohh…okay. I have some juice in my bag, should I bring it for you?" he enquired.

Ranga smiled, patted Raghu on his arm and said, "No, thank you, kanna. I'll be alright."

"Okay," Raghu said as he turned to leave for class. "What's

your name?" Ranga asked.

"Raghu," he replied. "And you?" "Rangasamy!"

the old man said, smiling. "Bye, Ranga thatha.

See you later!"

In the years that followed, the two of them grew close. They never spoke anything outside of school. Raghu knew nothing about Ranga's personal life, but he always greeted him on school days. He would smile and share his snacks with Ranga. He would buy Samosas from the canteen and bring them to the old man.

After spending 35 years of waking up looking forward to seeing his wife's face, he now had a little boy's good morning wish to give him energy. That wish made him want to continue to go on with life, even without his beloved Lakshmi.

As he took a mental walk down memory lane on his way to work, Ranga walked to the school's office, collected an envelope of cash, and went to the gate looking for Raghu.

Raghu entered the school on his bicycle and screamed good morning as he turned his cycle into the parking spots along the inside of his school's main compound.

Ranga gestured to Raghu asking him to come to him.

"You know how you've given me samosas, biscuits, juices and so many other things in the past?"

"Yes?" Raghu seemed confused.

"Here is a little something from me, for you," Ranga said, handing an entire envelope of cash to Raghu.

"What is it?" "It's

my salary."

"I'm not taking your money," Raghu pushed Ranga's arm away.

"No. You need to listen to me. Today's my last day as a security guard at this school. I've always been nice to all the kids here, but nobody has been as nice to me as you have. I want you to have this. Buy something you like. Maybe a cycle with gears. That way, you will always remember me," Ranga said, struggling to keep his voice from shaking.

"You won't be here from tomorrow?" Raghu's voice sank a little.

"No."

"Okay. I'll take it. Thank you."

"Go to class now."

"Yes. Just one thing."

"What?"

"I'll miss seeing you every morning."

Ranga put his arm around Raghu's shoulder and said, "Me too, kanna. Me too."

"And I won't forget you."

Raghu left for class and Ranga left school before Raghu was done with his sessions.

Two weeks later, another security guard called Raghu and told him that Ranga had passed away in his sleep a few days earlier.

"Ohhh…," Raghu thought. He didn't know how to respond. He got home that evening and opened the envelope of cash Ranga gave him.

It had a small piece of paper inside which read, "thank you". Raghu put it back inside the envelope, placed it in his cupboard drawer, and wiped a tear off his cheeks.

"Rest in peace, Ranga thatha," he muttered.

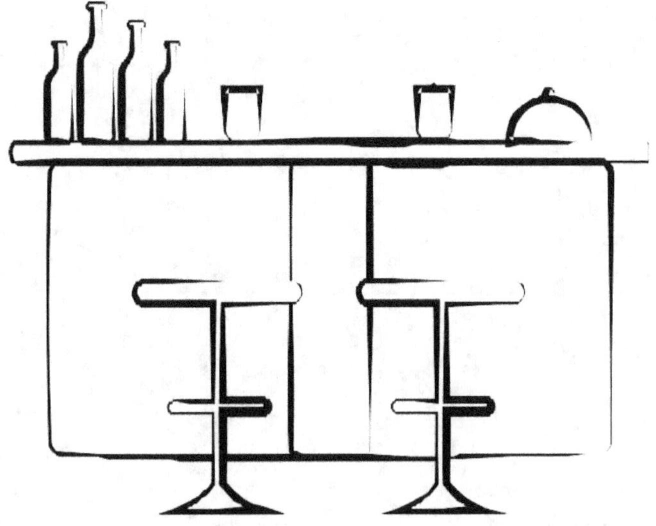

The perfeCT WeekenD

It was Friday night and Jeet was exhausted. He left the office and went right across the street to his usual weekend watering hole. He would sip a beer, buy a drink for a beautiful woman and go to her place. The next morning, he would be gone before she opened her eyes.

Unlike other Fridays, this particular night, he got hammered before he could make a move on anybody. But as fate would have it, he still found himself in bed with a woman (whose name he didn't remember) on his side. He checked his watch and sighed. 7:30AM. He checked his mobile and it was off. He quietly dressed himself and slipped out.

He got home, washed up and left to catch up with his gaming group. After spending the whole day killing people online, he went to his favourite bar, again. This time, he decided to not lose control over his drinking. Unfortunately, he found himself lying in the back of a van with a woman he didn't know. He tried to leave quietly, but the door squealed when he opened it.

"Shut it properly," said the woman as he left.

He walked to his place, took a shower, took a burger from the truck outside his place and left to meet his gaming gang.

"Today's Sunday and I need to get back home so I can be on time for work tomorrow," he thought.

He felt a little tipsy from the case of beer he chugged down. Just as he planned to leave and hit the bed, he saw a girl across the street check him out. He caught her eye. She smiled. He smiled back. Unsurprisingly, history repeated itself. The following morning, he woke up and found himself in an empty room with nothing but a note on his side.

"Veer, I need to leave early for work, please find your way home. Coffee is on the kitchen counter, if you'd like."

"Who the hell's Veer? Goodness, me! She must have been even more hammered than I was!" he thought.

He poured himself some coffee despite knowing he was over an hour late for work.

An hour later, he entered the office and made his way to his cabin.

"Sir"

"Sir"

People greeted him as he walked past them.

He saw the back of a girl's head as he entered his room.

"Are you the new assistant?" he asked.

"Yes, sir," she said as she turned, but he was already in his seat.

She walked in and froze two steps past the door.

Her eyes widened and her mouth, open just enough for a bee to have made its way in if it wished to.

"Oh! It's you," Jeet said, surprised but unruffled. The

girl stood there speechless.

"Thanks for the coffee," he continued.

She forced a smile and nodded awkwardly.

"This is unusual. I don't ever see a woman's face the afternoon after we're done. Looks like you and I are going to have to see each other everyday for a while."

Her eyes were glued to the floor.

"What's your name?" he enquired.

"Sorry?"

"Your name, please"

"Sara."

"Hi, Sara. I'm Jeet"

"Yes, sir. I know"

"Your note from earlier this morning read Veer." "I'm

sorry, sir. I must've misspelt."

"It's not a problem. Don't feel bad. Happens to the best of us"

Sara nodded and tried to leave the room. "Sara,

what's wrong with you?"

"Sorry, sir?"

"Why did you go home with a man 25 years older than you?"

"Sir…"

"It's alright. Whenever you're ready to talk, I'm ready to help."

"Sure, thank you," she said and walked out.

She was embarrassed by his question and the way he phrased it.

A few minutes later, she walked back into his cabin.

"Why did you agree to go home with a girl 25 years younger than you?"

Jeet looked up and smiled. "Bold!" he thought.

"When your wife of the same age leaves you for a man 20 years younger than you, this seems like the logical thing to do," he replied matter-of-factly and resumed work on his laptop.

Sara didn't know how to react. "I'm sorry," she muttered. Jeet couldn't hear it.

"I have a call now. Please close the door behind you," he ordered.

Sara left the room.

Meanwhile, on his laptop, Jeet clicked play on a video.

"Happy birthday to you. Happy birthday to you. Happy birthday my husband, happy birthday to you," sang a middle-aged woman.

Later that evening, as he left for home, he turned to Sara and asked her what she was paying for her place.

"15,000.""Why don't you take my place and pay me that same rent? I'll move into your place."

"Sir?"

"My place is closer to the office. It's fully furnished. You will have multiple balconies looking over the sea. All you have to do is say yes and the place is yours."

"Really?"

"Do I look like I'm joking?" "If

you're serious, I'm okay"

"Great. I'll be down in the parking lot. Black Gloster. 0107. Find me"

"Today?!" she asked, surprised.

"No time like the present!" Jeet declared and walked away.

"Why do you want to give away a place that overlooks the sea?"

"It's haunted."

"Sorry?"

"For me. Not for you. Don't worry. You will love the place. My wife had exquisite taste."

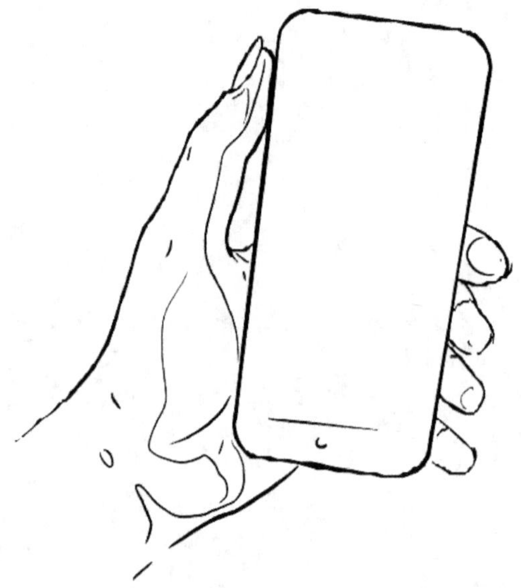

The SerIAl SCrOller

It was a marathon week. Anurag had just gotten out of office after launching a critical product for his company's high-profile client. After months of 80-hour weeks, he knuckled down for a 100-hour week to help close the launch. He was exhausted.

Right before he left the office, his manager walked in and handed him a letter. His hard work was rewarded with a Promotion. A handsome pay rise, lesser working hours and better benefits! There was a little bit of energy hiding behind the giant structure of exhaustion.

He took a rickshaw to his place and opened Swiggy on his mobile phone. He placed an order for 2 butter naans and one methi malai mutter. It was a ritual. At the end of every good day, he would order it from his favourite Punjabi restaurant. If it was a bad day, he would order a thin crust cheese burst from Mojo's pizza. Food played both roles in his life: celebratory partner and the shoulder he leaned on when required.

The past few months had taken a heavy toll on him physically, but he also felt emotionally weary. Two-minute phone calls with his parents and memes on Instagram with his friends weren't enough to keep his spirits up. Energy leaked consistently, but he felt like there was no refill in sight. But the promotion changed it. He decided to call his friends and catch up after what seemed like an eternity. He reached home and took a long hot shower. He then had his dinner with a sitcom playing on his TV. Not a new sitcom, just the same old How I Met your Mother episodes running over and over again, every evening before he fell asleep on his couch. He didn't use his bedroom; it was as if his mattress and cot didn't exist. He ate on the sofa, worked on the sofa and slept on the sofa. With newfound energy from the delicious buttery meal he just devoured, he swiped his mobile open.

He dialled his best friend's number from the dial-pad. Didn't need the contacts for that one! He had known the number by heart since he was 10.

Tring tring…

Tring tring…

Tring tring…

"The user you're trying to reach is currently busy. Please try again later," said the automated voice on the other side of the call.

He dialled his mother's number next. She seemed to be in a hurry. "Anurag, there are guests here. The kitchen is a big mess. Have you eaten? Eat and go to sleep soon. Sleep well. I'll talk to you tomorrow."

In 20 seconds, she disconnected the call and went back to her work. He felt awkward.

"She didn't even ask me about the product launch… she didn't give me a chance of telling her about the promotion either," he thought.

He heaved a sigh of…something. He didn't know what it was. It was only Friday and the whole weekend lay ahead of him. And it was supposed to be a weekend of celebration. He had finally put an end to a project that had taken away all his time and energy. He wanted to mark its completion by sharing it with people he loved. To add to his initial plan, he also discovered he was being promoted. The weekend's significance shifted several notches upward. Unfortunately for him, all the ones he loved lived in different cities. He couldn't meet them to convey the news; he had to call. But they weren't available. Out of sight, out of mind, right?

His thoughts ran him ragged.

"What do I do this weekend? How do I celebrate this moment? How do I make this weekend memorable? I've been under the pump for so long! I deserve rest. I deserve peace. I deserve to feel happy!"

"You are not going to let my weekend slip away. You will find a way out of this!" said a voice from inside him.

He quickly opened Whatsapp on his mobile and began scrolling. He would find someone to talk to if he scrolled long enough. At least, that was the idea. He went through tens of different group chats that were muted - groups with office colleagues, old school and college batch groups, project groups with stakeholders, etc. There were hardly any individual chats visible on his screen. He wasn't the messaging type—he wasn't even the talking type. He was content with talking to just his mother and his best friend, both of whom were busy that night. He scrolled and scrolled; he passed names of people who were good friends, but not enough for him to share this moment with. He dug deeper by going to his contacts and went from A to Z. Cousins, friends, colleagues, old mentors, but no name popped out of his screen and called out to him.

After an hour of running his thumb up and down the mobile screen, he decided to give up. There was nobody else worth sharing this moment with, so he chose to wait and share it with his mother and best friend the following morning.

"It's just you and me, old friend," he said, as he clicked play on the How I Met Your Mother icon on his Hotstar account.

"It's just you and me tonight."

He heaved a sigh, again. Heavier this time, as he thought back to all the previous times he felt empty at the end of a tedious project. Scrolling had become an ugly habit.

He wasn't looking at the TV screen, but he heard Barney Stinson in his signature style say, "Whatever you do in this life…it's not legendary unless your friends are there to see it."

He turned to the TV, paused for a second before closing his eyes and taking a deep breath.

"So much for Friday night!"

l~IfT~ & l~AnD~

I'm a traveller. Not by nature, but by work. My job needs me to go to random places and meet different people and survey them on behalf of large organisations. I get to meet the most amazing people in the process and I'm thankful for that. Since these companies pay us big bucks, I also have the luxury of staying in good places and eating great food. Everything is reimbursed and I can splurge on food and accommodation if I feel like it.

But there's one feeling that has recently found its way to the inside of my head. I've been doing this for years and not once have I ever felt this before. Most times, my travel involves a combination of air-rail or air-road transport. This feeling occurs most when I'm at the airport waiting to board a flight. Once I complete my security check, have my food at the lounge and go to my gate, I get this sensation. Something that resembles sadness in the subtlest of ways. I don't know why.

Once I'm at the gate, there's usually 45 minutes before boarding begins. There's another 20-25 minutes in the flight between boarding and lift-off. In this hour, my mind reminds me of how there's nobody who knows where I'm going and when I'm landing. Nobody texts or calls me to ask if I'm on time, if I've grabbed a bite to eat before the flight, if I've landed safely, if I've reached my hotel, if I'm too tired with all the surveys. There's just nobody whose day involves the process of thinking about me and what I'm doing.

It's probably my fault. I never really developed relationships that could grow to that level. It's ironic, right? For someone whose job depends on building relationships (however short) with people to understand their views on issues, I suck at relationships outside of work. I have no friends, no boyfriend, and no family after my parents passed away…I'm well and truly on my own.

What's weird is the fact that I did not realise it bothered me. I've always enjoyed being on my own…until recently. Now, I'm suddenly feeling the need to have someone to talk to, laugh with and be happy around. I want someone to ask me what I'm doing, how I'm doing, where I'm going, when I'm coming back, if I'm free to talk for a while…

I'm not sure if I'm craving a boyfriend or just a friend. But I know I need someone to share these little joys with. And my fears. God knows I have them. Maybe that will help keep this feeling away. Maybe.

huSbAnDS AnD hAbITS

Every morning, we had a routine. My husband and I used to sit at our table and have a cup of tea together. We would discuss the news, what our kids were doing, politics, business…anything and everything under the sun. It was my favourite part of the day and although he never actually said it to me explicitly in words, I believe he loved it as much as I did.

This day last year, he passed away from a cardiac arrest in the middle of the night. He was gone before either of us knew what was happening. His heart stopped beating, all of a sudden. Without notice, without any sign.

In the year since his demise, I've continued to keep up my end of the routine. I made 2 cups of tea, placed them both on the table. The difference? There weren't as many words as before and only one cup was empty when we were done.

I've learned to live on, actually. I learned embroidery, I jog every morning, I get together with my neighbours every weekend for some old lady fun, I watch movies, I read a book a day and I mean my smile. I don't fake it anymore.

No matter what though, I can't seem to give up the

morning ritual. Does that mean I'm not okay? Does that mean I'm still hung up on what was? Or is it just an old habit?

I know he's not here anymore and I can't really call him mine. But it's like this song…

You're not mine anymore…but I'm still a little bit yours…

mOTherS AnD mOrnInG COffeeS

I'm a coffee master. I won't say my coffee is the best you will ever have, but I will say this. You will not forget my coffee once you taste it (for good reasons). It really will give you everything you expect from a coffee too. You want calmness? It will calm you down while simultaneously giving you the energy to go again, if needed. You want a warm hug? It will hug you hard enough to melt your heart. Everyone who has ever visited my home has said, at least once, "Aabha! Your coffee is aaammmaazzzzinngggg!"

The funny thing though, I can't drink my own coffee. I love coffee. I've been having it for as long as I can remember. My mother used to bring me coffee every morning until I was home.

So, naturally, the first thing I learned once I left home for my job was to make my mother's coffee the exact same way. Measured to milligrams. It tasted good, but it wasn't the same. So, I tried everything. I bought a different type of milk, altered the amount of coffee and sugar, the temperature…everything. But my coffee just didn't give me what I needed.

In the process of learning how to make myself a cup of coffee that soothed me, I ended up knowing how to make a coffee that soothed everybody but me. Now, I run a small side-hustle (that's what they call it nowadays, right?). I call it *The Morning Coffee*; I basically make coffee and sell it online to boys or girls who are away from home and need a good cup of coffee.

But every day, there's really only one thing I think about. When will I get to have my mother's morning coffee next? There is something in her coffee that mine will never have. Maybe it's the milk. Maybe it's the mug she serves it in. Or maybe, it's her. It's the sight of her in the morning when your mind is asking you to go back to bed and escape the day for a little while longer. It's the smile she serves it with…the love she pours it with…the warmth she brings it with. It's everything about her.

This is my conclusion. It was never about the coffee. It was, is and always will be, about the person who gave me that coffee. It is about the person who gave meaning to my coffee. I can't believe it took my dumb brain so many years to figure this out.

Whenever, Wherever

"Is that Shivani?" Vishnu left his seat and took a few steps to have a better look.

"Are you mad? Why will she be in Chennai?" Sanjay dismissed him.

"I don't know, it looked like her for a second," Vishnu said as he occupied his seat.

"It's been a long time, man. I think it's time you stopped looking for her in places you won't find her. Actually, it's time for you to stop looking for her anywhere."

"I don't look for her at all. She finds me."

"Oh, come on. How will she find you when she's not even there?"

Vishnu leaned forward and put his palms together.

"It's like this. I'm sure it's going to sound stupid to you. But it is what it is and I can't control it. I'll try and explain it to you. If you get it, great. If you don't, wait until you're in love and then you will understand."

"Okay, then."

"So, this girl I just saw and left the table…she wasn't facing our side; I could only see the back of her head. But her hair was long and wavy, yet soft. Just like Shivani's. She was not too thin, but just right. Like Shivani. She was tall…practically our height. Again, like Shivani!"

"There are thousands of people who will fit this description, Vishnu. What's your point?"

"That's exactly my point. That's my problem! There are so many people who bear her resemblance. And that's torturing me. Couldn't she have been one of a kind? Like Aishwarya Rai or something? In that case, I would've never been able to compare any other girl to her. Why did she have to be so much like a girl next door?"

"I have a counter question. Why do you have to be so much of a moron?"

"No! You don't understand. I swear I'm not constantly searching for her. You think I don't know she's not in Chennai? You think I don't know that she's in Bangalore with her sister? You think I don't know she hates yellow and will never wear the top that girl is currently wearing? You think I don't know she won't wear earrings that are large and shiny like those? You think I don't know all of this? I do! I do, very very well! But it doesn't help. My brain, for some reason, puts all that information aside when my eyes catch someone who shares her features. It's so horrible. You must be inside me to see how pathetic it makes me feel."

"I'm sorry if I was being insensitive. I understand…but it's been 6 years. At some point, you will have to take responsibility for refusing to let yourself move on and accept that she's not yours anymore."

"She is not mine. I know."

"Why have you not dated anyone else since your breakup?"

"Dating makes it sound so casual. Shivani and I didn't date. We were in a relationship."

"Okay. Why have you not had any other relationships since then?"

"I don't know. I just didn't feel like I wanted another one."

"Until you have another one, you will remain stuck in your memories. You will continue to project your mental images of her onto every other female crossing your path."

"You're right. But the problem is with me. I know all of this, but I can't bring myself to do anything about it."

"Do you feel lonely?"

"More often than I like to admit."

"What do you do when you're craving that company?"

"I think of how I never felt lonely when we were still a couple."

"You never tried speaking to another girl? Swiped on dating apps?"

"I did. I told you when I tried to put myself out there. I could never build a conversation with anybody."

"Did you ever go on a date with anyone?" "No."

"Why not?"

"I didn't want to."

"What's your outlet then? How do you get past that feeling of being alone?"

"I don't know. It passes. I don't really do anything about it. The feeling comes in waves and leaves in waves. Outside of those waves, I'm pretty happy. I'm doing great at work, I'm enjoying my time at home with my family. I'm totally okay."

"That's good to hear. But are you happy?" "I

am."

"Sure?"

"Yes. I'm sure."

"How can you be happy if you're feeling lonely?"

"Loneliness is a feeling. Happiness is a feeling. You're not happy everyday, right? I'm not lonely everyday either."

"But how will you be truly happy without finding a partner who will give you what Shivani gave you?"

"I'll be glad if it happens to me. But as of now, it hasn't. And I'm okay with that too. My life is pretty good even without that partner thing."

WOulD yOu DO IT AGAIn?

I'm at a hill station now, rain is pouring down as if all of Earth's thirst is to be quenched today. The branches are bouncing, green leaves are dancing, and the cold wind is blowing with all its might. I'm sitting on the balcony of my hotel room, listening to soothing music with a hot mug of coffee in my hand. There's surely no better setting to spend an evening after a few hectic weeks at work, right?

But there's a catch. Whenever I visit a hill station, whenever I'm atop the mountains, my mind plays the same set of movies in my head. It revisits the same memories and reopens the door to old feelings I don't even remember that well anymore.

Okay, who am I kidding? I remember them like they happened yesterday. So, in this episode of "Back to the hills", we're going to bring you back once again for a guest appearance. It's not really a guest appearance when you occupy a permanent place in my head, but let's call it that because it makes me sound a little less pathetic.

I'm wondering why on earth hill stations remind me of you, but I have no idea whatsoever. Maybe it's because my life reached its happiness peak during my time with you, or maybe it's because I'm an idiot who reminds himself of you and then searches for a rationale when there isn't any.

We're over a 1000 kms away—we haven't spoken in what feels like aeons, we're surely beyond the point in our lives where we matter to each other. But it's so stupid that I still hope we do. Not always, just sometimes. Times like this, when you flood my mind and drown all my other thoughts, all I can think about is if you still remember me occasionally. And if yes, do you remember me fondly? If yes, does the thought of me bring a smile to your glorious face? If yes, does my absence feel a bit too apparent in those moments? If yes, does that trigger a tear or two from those big, beautiful eyes? If yes, do you feel grateful to have met me? If yes, would you do it all over again if we had the chance?

Will You?

If you know the world is going to end tomorrow, will you call me? Will you ask to meet me?

And when you see me, will you hug me? Will you be glad to be in the same space as me? Will you unleash that atom bomb of a smile at me? Will you choose to spend your last few hours on this earth with me? Will you finally unburden yourself from the expectations the world has of you and just let yourself be with me?

Will you love me the way you always wanted to? Will you hold me hard enough and long enough to see if the broken pieces of my heart can be healed? Will you hold my hand and draw circles on top of my thumb with yours? Will you see the pain in my eyes and listen to how unkind the past few years have been to me? Will you place me on your lap and wipe off my tears? Will you kiss my forehead? Will you run your beautiful fingers through my rough and scanty hair as I fall asleep?

Will you think back to all the times we calmed each other with nothing but silence? Will you look at me in my sleep and be grateful for having someone you could understand (and who could understand you) without any words at all? Will you tell me you love me? Will you wake me up early so we could watch the sun rise, for the first and last time together? Will you lean on my shoulder, put your arms in mine and wait patiently until you breathe your last breath with me?

I know I will.

Will you?

What We Talk About When We Talk About Loneliness

lOnG DISTAnCe

I go to the supermarket to pick up some stuff. A boy places a pack of chips on the top shelf and asks his girlfriend to take it. He walks away laughing and she runs behind to slap him on his back. They fool around like this the entire time. They're young and in love. It's beautiful to see.

The following day, I go to a restaurant to have dinner. My partner's not here with me, so I decided to go solo. I see couples around me, smiling and having a nice dinner with each other. I order and share a picture of my girlfriend's favourite butter chicken with her. As I take my first bite, I receive a red heart reply on the picture.

"I wish you were here with me," I type. I

delete it and type something else. *"When*

are you coming here?"

I hit send.

"The Eid Weekend," is the reply.

It's about a month away. "That's

too long," I think.

"Can't wait!" I type and hit send.

"Me too" came the response. "Video call me when you get home," she added.

"What other work do I have?" I replied.

The conversation ended with another red heart emoticon.

As nice as it is to see couples around me, it also makes me a wee bit sad.

Sad that she isn't here with me to feel that same love of proximity that these people are feeling. My girlfriend and I don't play around like kids in the supermarket— we don't go out to dinner often. We stay home and order in. We talk for a while and then just do our own thing. But that feeling of being in the same space as her is something that I can't fully explain.

We've been in different cities for a year now and that feeling of missing her presence is more apparent now than ever before.

As I scroll Instagram, I see a video where Kavya from Little Things says, "I'm tired of seeing you in these rectangles, Dhruv. Why aren't you here?"

I send it to her with a message, *"Why aren't you here?"*

"You're the one who flew off to Delhi because your company was willing to promote you. So please don't come crying now," she replied.

I low-key regret moving here. I don't get to see her often, I don't get briyani the way I like, tickets to Bangalore are bloody expensive, and don't even get me started on the weather of our national capital.

I have half a heart to book tickets right now for this weekend and go see her. But it would instantly burn a hole in my wallet that would take months to fill. So, I'll wait.

I'll wait a month to see her. I'll

wait a month to hold her.

I'll wait a month for her to hold me.

I'll wait a month to spend one whole weekend in her presence.

And then, I'll watch as she flies back to Bangalore. And then, I'll wait again. For a month...maybe two.

Until we meet again. And the cycle repeats and repeats and repeats again...

And I keep reminding myself that it's okay to wait... and wait...and wait again...until there's no need to wait anymore.

But sometimes, I can't wait for this waiting to end.

The hOuSewIfe

The alarm goes off at 6AM. I turn it off and push my blanket away. I brush my teeth, making as little noise as possible and go to the kitchen.

After half an hour of cutting vegetables and prepping for breakfast, I go and wake my daughter up. I return to the kitchen to finish the cooking before she's ready so I can braid her hair and get her to leave for school on time.

Just as she comes out of her bath, I wake my husband up with his coffee. As he finishes his coffee, my daughter has her breakfast while I braid her hair.

Once it's done, my husband drops her off at school.

He returns and washes up to leave for office. He has his breakfast, kickstarts his bike and makes his way to an office not too far from home.

Once they leave, I have my breakfast, get the lunch ready and rest for a while.

My husband returns home later to pick up his lunch around 1:30PM. But before that, at 12:30, I walk to my daughter's school to hand over hers.

Once I return from handing my daughter her lunch, I take a cold shower and eat my lunch. Once my husband collects his lunch, I lock the front door and go to sleep. I wake up and wait for my daughter to come home so I can feed her some snacks.

She sits for a brief 20 minutes as she has her biscuits as I have my coffee. Then, she turns on the TV and gets lost in movies.

My husband comes home, has his coffee and continues to work on his laptop. The three of us spend an entire evening exchanging not more than 50 words between each other.

I try initiating conversations with my daughter, but she asks me to stay quiet.

"Let me watch the movie, ma!" she says.

I ask my husband if we can do something together over the weekend; something like a day out with our daughter at a park or a movie plus dinner outing. But he's rarely up for it.

"You have the whole week to rest at home. I have just the weekend. So, please don't ask me to come out," he says.

~

They love dosas. So I make them crisp dosas every night with different chutneys. They eat it and go back to what they're doing. I return and eat my dinner alone by the table with the TV noise still playing loudly in the background.

Then, I give my daughter some milk and get her to bed. I clear up the kitchen, lock the doors and go to bed. My husband generally comes to sleep much later. I'm often too tired to stay beyond 10:30 or 11PM.

I check if the alarm is on and shut my eyes.

~

The next morning, the alarm goes off. And the day repeats like clockwork.

During the day, I spend about an hour trying to catch up with my mother and my friends.

The rest of the time, I wait for my husband and daughter, hoping to do something with them. Not something outdoorsy, just something simple like having a conversation about their day at the office and school. I try and ask about her friends and his work and his team at the office. I ask if they had a good day. My enquiries are usually met with nods of the head or one-word replies.

It has been 12 years now and the frequency of my enquiries has reduced. But their responses remain non-existent.

Sometimes, I ask my other friends who are stay- at-home wives and their days are eerily similar. Heartbreakingly similar. A few of them tell me their children make an effort to spend time with them. I'm happy for them. Some say that the kids grow further away as they get older until they leave home. And then they start getting attentive. That means I have another 10-12 years before my daughter notices me.

Nobody seems to have an idea when the husbands notice their wives. My mother once jokingly said, "after we die". It didn't feel like a joke to me, even though she was laughing pretty hard while saying that.

"This is the life of a housewife, my dear," was allshe said to console me.

I realise it is. I just don't understand why.

WAS I The reASOn yOu DIDn'T lOve AGAIn?

" Hey, Anita! What a surprise! Why didn't you tell me you were coming?"

He seems very happy to see me. So, I hug him. I am not as pleased to see him because there's something on my mind. I'm here to get it cleared with him.

"I need to ask you something," I say and pause before continuing. "Can we talk?"

"Of course! Don't you want something to drink first?"

"No", I reply sternly.

"Alright. Is everything okay?"

"It's not. I'm going to ask you a lot of questions, and I want you to be completely honest with me."

"I'm always honest with you. So, it's not going to be a problem. Tell me. What do you want to know?"

I am not in the mood to beat around the bush. I'm going to jump right into it. I feel uncomfortable. A little scared, too.

"Am I the reason you never loved again? Did you choose not to marry again because I didn't want you to remarry?" I ask in one breath, terrified of the answer awaiting me.

What if he says yes? I'm going to feel so horrible about myself. Why did I choose to play such a risky game? I'm an idiot. I'm the biggest idiot to ever set foot on earth.

"Ani, it's not that simple–", he starts.

"It's a simple question. Just answer with a yes or no. That's all I'm looking for," I interrupt before he could go on a tangent. I appear calm, but I'm freaking out inside.

My dad sighs. "Not all questions in life can be answered in binaries. So, if you're looking for a yes or no, I'm sorry because you're going to be disappointed."

I don't know what to say. I heave a sigh of partial frustration.

"On the other hand, if you really want to know why I did not marry again, I can tell you why."

"Okay, go on."

"Great. You go freshen up. I'll make us some lunch," he says, ruffling my hair.

I want to hug him and apologise. I also want to slap him hard on his back and scream at him. But I can't seem to bring myself to do either.

"Okay" is all I can utter in response.

I take my bag and disappear to my room. I see old pictures on my bedside table and the wall opposite my bed. I see pictures of him carrying me on our front lawn, me painting his face with Chelsea blue, him playing football with me, and more pictures from my childhood. But was he really happy in any of those pictures? Or was he pretending? That's what I need to know. That's what I'm here to find out. I know I'm selfish, but I want to know if my selfishness affected his happiness.

I go back to the living room an hour later and I see him reading a book.

"Can you tell me the reason?"

He puts the book down and looks up at me.

"Is everything alright with you? You don't seem okay." "I

will be, once you tell me the reason."

"Are you sure about that?"

"No, I'm not," I reply quietly before looking at him, determined. "But I do know that I need to know."

"Okay, go grab us a couple of plates. We can discuss this over lunch."

We start to eat and he begins.

"I could've married again if I wanted to, but I wasn't ever sure it was the right thing to do. If I did, maybe I would've decided to go ahead and do it."

"Was there someone who you felt could've been the one to marry?"

"No."

"Don't lie. Please be honest. I remember…there was someone and from whatever I remember, you did like her quite a bit."

"It wasn't meant to be."

"Maybe it would've been, if I hadn't created a scene and forced you to quit seeing her, right?"

"Anita, listen to me. You are not the reason I am on my own. It's my own choice "

"Oh please, dad. Give me a break! I know I'm the reason. I was such a horrible daughter to you. I quit talking to you for years after I knew you were trying to replace mom."

"I was never looking to replace your mother. I was only looking for someone to help me with my life."

"I understand that now! But back then, I was so mad at you. I hated you so much. I know how mean I was to you. I would slam the door in your face, act out when you tried to tell me things, do everything that I knew you didn't like…" I trail off. There is no point in bringing all those moments up. I just need to make up for them. "I'm so sorry, dad. When I lost my mother, you lost your wife. And I never really looked at it that way. I'm so sorry…" I manage to force out before running to my room.

All parents would normally call out the kid's name and follow them. My dad was different. He never followed me—he waited for me to come to him.

After a while, I notice a paper slide in from under the door.

"I'm in the hall for whenever you're ready to continue the conversation," read the note.

Why does he have to be so nice? Why can't he slap me or scream at me like I've done to him countless times?

"There's chocolate ice cream outside the door. Take it before it melts."

I take my ice cream and eat it all in my room. I don't have the courage to look him in the eye. All my life, I've complained about parents ruining the lives of their kids. But today, I feel like I ruined his.

More than an hour later, I find him asleep on the couch. I get a notification on my phone and see that Chelsea's Premier League match has just begun. I turn on the TV and notice his cracked heels. I bring my moisturiser and wake him up.

"It's time for your match," I announce. "Oh,

yeah. I forgot."

"Since when do you forget Chelsea football?"

"Since the time watching them play became as hard as staying away from you."

"So, now, you're staying without them and me?" Dad

just shrugs. "Something like that, yeah."

"Your feet look terrible, do you not take care of them?"

"Aahh, they're okay!" he says, dismissing skin-care like it's nothing.

"Dad…"

"Let me sit up, Ani. I'll explain."

"No. Let me apply moisturiser to these horrible feet. You can tell me lying down."

"Okay, listen. I didn't enjoy how you went off on me when you found out I was seeing someone. I definitely didn't enjoy you alienating me from your life. But that's a thing of the past. If I felt strongly that I needed someone other than you, I would've told you that and brought someone into our lives. But I didn't because I knew you were enough for me. You were, are and always will be everything I need. Do you understand?"

"Promise?"

He throws his legs out the couch and hugs me. "I

promise", he says, kissing my head.

"But everybody needs somebody, and you had nobody after mom."

"For a while, I felt like I needed someone. But that feeling faded with time. Don't you burden yourself with any of this. It was my choice to be alone. Actually, I was never alone. I had you, always."

I lean on his shoulder, neither of us looking at each other. Silence takes over.

"Being alone is being in solitude. Feeling alone is loneliness. I may have been alone, but I was never lonely."

I close my eyes. A little while later, I wake up to find the post-match interview of the Chelsea match running on TV.

~

Now I'm 10 years older than I was when I fell asleep watching the Chelsea match. He isn't by my side anymore. There's no food on the table, no paper notes slid under my door, nobody hugging me, nobody forgiving me when I'm mean, nobody standing by me irrespective of what I do.

I look at his picture hanging on the wall next to my mother's, tears stinging my eyes.

"I'm sorry, pa."